THE MAN WHO DIDN'T WASH HIS DISHES

A Parents Magazine Read Aloud and Easy Reading Program® Selection.

Distributed in Canada by Clarke, Irwin & Co., Ltd.
Toronto, Canada

The Man Who
Didn't Wash His Dishes

BY PHYLLIS KRASILOVSKY

ILLUSTRATED BY BARBARA COONEY

Parents Magazine Press
New York

ISBN: 0-385-07735-1 Trade
0-385-06353-9 Prebound

10   9   8   7   6   5   4   3   2   1

For
KATHY JEAN LUBART
and all the other children

There once was a man who lived all alone in a little house on the edge of a town. He didn't have any wife or children, so he always cooked his own supper, cleaned the house by himself, and made his own bed.

One night he came home hungrier than usual,

so he made himself a big, big supper.

It was a very good supper

(he liked to cook and could

make good things to eat),

but there was so much of it

that he grew very, very tired

by the time he'd finished.

He just sat back in his chair,

as full as he could be, and

decided he'd leave the dishes

till the next night, and then

he would wash them all at once.

But the next night he was TWICE as hungry,

so he cooked TWICE as big a supper,

and took TWICE as long to eat it,

and was TWICE as tired by the time

he'd finished.

So he left THOSE dishes in the sink, too.

Well, as the days went by he got hungrier and hungrier, and more and more tired, and so he never washed his dishes. After a while there were so MANY dirty dishes that they didn't all fit in the sink. So he began to pile them on the table.

Soon the table was so full that he

began to put them on his bookshelves.

And when THEY were full, he put them

just everywhere he could find an empty place.

Soon he had them all piled on the floor, too.

In fact, the floor got to be so FULL of dishes

that he had a hard time

getting into his house at night—

THEY WERE EVEN PILED AGAINST THE DOOR!

Then one night he looked in
his closet and found that
there WASN'T ONE CLEAN
DISH LEFT! He was hungry
enough to eat out of anything,
so he ate out of the soap dish
from the bathroom. It was
too dirty for him to use
again the NEXT night, so
he used one of his ash trays.

Pretty soon he had used up

all his ash trays. THEN

he ate out of some clean

flowerpots he found down

the cellar. When THEY

were all used up, he ate

out of his candy dishes and

drank water from vases.

He used up EVERYTHING finally—

even the pots he cooked his food in,

and he didn't know what to do! He

was SOOOO unhappy. His whole house

was full of dirty dishes—and dirty

flowerpots—and dirty ash trays—

and dirty candy dishes—and dirty

pots—and a dirty soap dish. He

couldn't even find his books—or

his alarm clock—or even his BED

any more! He couldn't sit down to

think because even his chairs were

filled with dishes, and he couldn't

find the sink so he could wash them!

But THEN—all of a sudden—IT BEGAN TO RAIN!

And the man got an idea.

He drove his big truck around to the side of the

house and piled all the dishes—and all the vases—

and all the flowerpots—and all the ash trays—

and all the candy dishes—

and the soap dish—on it,

and drove the truck

out into the rain.

The rain fell on everything and soon they were

clean again. THE RAIN HAD WASHED THEM!

Then the man carried everything back into the house again. He put the dishes in the dish closet, the pots in the pot closet, the ash trays on the tables, the candy dishes on the shelves, the flowerpots in the cellar, the vases where the vases go, and the soap dish in the bathroom.

He was so very, very tired after carrying everything back and putting it away that he decided that from then on he would always wash his dishes just as soon as he had finished his supper.

The next night when he came home he cooked his supper, and — when he had finished eating it — he washed the dishes and put them right away. He did this every night after that, too.

He is very happy now. He can find his chairs, and he can find his alarm clock, and he can find his BED. It is easy for him to get into his house, too, because there are no more dishes piled on the floor —— or anywhere!